DANGEROUSLY DISOBEYING DADDY

BY
AIYSHA SWALLOWGREN

ISBN 978-0-9984840-6-8
First Printing May 2022
Printed in United States of America

Contents

ACT

She loved how I would always act
So sweetly I knew just the exact
Way to get her body to react
I used my large frame to back
Her against the wall and the impact
Of my firm hands, the way she would act
Grabbing her throat and keeping eye contact
The rougher I got, the wetter she got, that's a fact
That she loves the way I forcefully attack
Her butt, it's very small and compact
She's getting damp thinking of how I smacked
Her ass so hard and fed her a snack
Of my nuts in her mouth my ballsack
Is full, her innocence is just an act

ALONE

What would happen if you were all alone
With me, you'd smell my cologne
Going after my dick like a dog and a bone
She hops on my lap and it makes her moan
She is touching herself reading this on her phone
She wants her mind totally blown
She had never been so roughly thrown
But those hard ass slaps make her moan
Her nipples so erect they have grown
Very sensitive smack, smack she starts to groan
Hew whole body is an erogenous zone
She likes when I'm aggressive and my tone
Is forceful, she makes me as hard as stone
I'm going to destroy you when we are alone

BEAT

I know she needs someone to firmly beat
Her body, she makes me wanna eat
Her through her panties and make her leak
She says Daddy you make it hurt so sweet
Collared slut loves it when I really beat
Her she's such a nasty freak
She'll do anything to taste my treat
I'm beating it up and making lots of heat
I'm making her soak her sheets
She's touching herself again, she's so weak
I'll beat her seven days a week
Walking her around collared on a crowded street
She wants all my dick, the complete
Package special delivery making her overheat
She's gagging for good dick, it's so sweet
I make her so horny and I'm discrete
Discretion and creativity is a hard combination to beat

BLACK

She calls me naughty, that's the pot calling the kettle black
As I lick the small of her back
My tongue is sliding down her asscrack
You make me the naughtiest, that's a fact
Especially in your mask of leather sexy black
I'll fill your entire counter with sexy MAC
I'm licking and nibbling your incredible rack
You're so horny that you start to smack
Your own ass until it's blue and black
I'm sipping your juices like fine cognac
You are bucking on me like it's horseback
She whispers Daddy go bareback
I'm eating her ass for a midnight snack
She just swallowed my entire ballsack
She drives me around in her Cadillac
It's sitting on chrome and shiny black

CARE

She said will you take care
Of me, I'll start pulling your hair
Ripping your hot little underwear
I'll do things nobody else would ever dare
I'll take care of you, beware
Little girl of this wolf are you aware
That there will be no mercy, I won't spare
You any pain, it's my pleasure to care
For you how you love the best I declare
You're going with me to the middle of nowhere
There's no way your body to prepare
You're a rabbit and I'm a polar bear
I'm going to choke you, so little air
Left, you love sucking on my huge pair
Of balls, you lick them with such care

CHAIN

She's collared and hands me the chain
She begs Daddy please bring the pain
You make me so wet my brain
Explodes Daddy tonight be my flame
She's dripping everywhere and begins to exclaim
You lift me up like an airplane
You make me squirt everywhere like champagne
Daddy you're a sex lion that broke his chain
I'm Tarzan and tonight you're Jane
Dragging you by the hair gets you high like cocaine
I'm making her as wet as a hurricane
The things I do to her are quite profane
But she never says no or complains
Good little slut now lick my cum off the chain

CHEERLEADER

I have the hottest little cheerleader
She's a sexy unicorn like creature
I really wish I was her teacher
And she needed to pass, so she I can eat her
Would you like your pussy eaten hot little cheerleader?
I'm grabbing your hair and dragging you under the bleachers
Slide your bloomers to the side, show me your beaver
Start rubbing yourself now, hot and horny cheerleader.

Confess

He knew that she desired to confess
Her desires she wouldn't express
Her desires so he made an educated guess
You love it dark and dirty yes
She gulped yes sir I do and she will confess
Urges to be naughty and filthy are hard to suppress
She had a desire to shock and impress
It got her so excited she started to caress
Herself and his words made her a hot mess
With his encouragement came progress
She starts getting hot as she sweats
She trusted him, she trusted the process
The nastiest fantasies she would openly confess

CONSENT

Last night I dreamed of consent
While you were laying there I dreamt
Of fully releasing my anger all pent
Up energy, I grabbed you and bent
You over and started to physically vent
You cried and said no, I don't consent
But I kept going and started to torment
Your body, you begged me to relent
But it made my resolve and intent
Stronger my anger into your body went
So hard the bruises became frequent
I covered your mouth, no argument
You never knew the extent of my depravity, the extent
Of my insanity until I ignored consent

CREAMING

I love when you get so excited you start creaming
I want to drink your juices as I slowly start eating
You making you feel so hot you are needing
To explode I will make you see colors like you are dreaming
I want to get you so hot, I want you overheating
I want you to touch yourself until you start screaming
Fuck yes sir, you are why I am creaming
I want to make you so happy you start weeping
You deserve a man in your life devoted to pleasing
Your wildest fantasies imagine my hands creeping
Along your lower back as I whisper you love creaming
Don't you filthy slut I enjoy keeping
You on the edge of your seat with a puddle from your leaking
I treat you like a queen and when you start queefing
That's when you start uncontrollably creaming

CREAMY

She said please Daddy I'm getting creamy
She said please make me feel dreamy
She's addicted to how leaky
I make her, she's the most freaky
She loves surprising me, she's so sneaky
Daddy please I need you to completely
Fuck me I'm so horny and creamy
She reaches for my dick, she's so greedy
She's rubbing her magic lamp, I'm her genie
She's so wet and her fingers are so squeaky
She whispers you make me so steamy
Getting her wet is super easy
I just have to dominate her extremely
She licks her fingers; this is so tasty and creamy

CUCKOLD

I'm going to make you wet when I cuckold
Your husband you like me to be bold
Like grab your tits and do what you are told
I'll make you so hot you'll beg for the cold
I'm deep in your ass looking for gold
You'll cheat on your husband as I cuckold
Him I'll cover you in the fanciest things sold
When God made you he broke the mold
I'll fuck you in every spot in your household
I'll choke you hard, you'll love my stranglehold
Your my filthiest bitch let me control
You bitch finger yourself and make him cuckold

DEGRADE

She asked if I'd be willing to degrade
Her dumb bitch I never delayed
Pull out your tits slut, she displayed
Them and I said there's only one thing you're made
For that's being a hole and she loved to trade
Her self-respect for me to properly degrade
Her worthless slut I absolutely afraid
Someone might find out I made her aid
Me in licking my toilet, fucking filthy maid
You're so useless the only grade
You deserve is an F for fucking depraved
She's a useless, slutty mermaid
Her secret was it made her explode like a grenade
Whenever I would roughly slap and degrade

Deliver

She said make me cum and I always deliver
Like UPS from the back I start to lick her
Getting drunk off her juices like liquor
She says do me dirty, treat me like pure
Filth, make me scream Daddy, so I deliver
Swift, firm slaps on her ass as her lips begin to quiver
She's a unicorn and my face is covered in glitter
What's sexy is when she starts to finger
Her tight asshole that's my favorite dinner
I'm going to stick my tongue so deep in her
Are you horny baby, did Daddy deliver?

DEPRAVED

She loved his nature, he's totally depraved
Nobody before had ever misbehaved
So magnificently the things he made
Her do and say really gave
Her a new definition of depraved
She slowly lifted her skirt showing her shaved
Flower and it made him totally crazed
He was fixated on her as she bathed
She knew how desperately he craved
To be allowed to not hide and he amazed
Her by the depth of how he's absolutely depraved

Desk

I'm hiding under her desk
She's sits down and I become a naughty pest
My tongue through her panties pressed
Firmly, she's like fuck you are making a hot mess
She's leaking so much under her desk
My tongue starts to gently molest
Her ass and she's like you're the best
She can't help squeezing her perfect breasts
I'm her pleasure prisoner, I'm not under arrest
I'm just over here licking her blessed
Body, she's got a treasure chest
Not many men make her leak while she's dressed
But I know where to lick and she expressed
There's a demon under my desk!

Dessert

She's so thirsty and hungry for my dick it's making her berserk
She bends over in the shortest skirt
Shaking her ass saying please really hurt
Me Daddy she's frantically starting to insert
Another finger in herself tasting her juices, tastes like desert
She's the filthiest, wettest pervert
I'm fingering her in the middle of a concert
Her nipples so hard and alert
I'm bending her over, railing her makes her squirt
I make her lick that filthy puddle, it's her just desserts

Dominate

I'd like to apply to dominate
You face down ass up that's great
Tie you up and let you wait
Lick every inch of you, make you satiate
Leaking out of your panties, you start to fixate
On Daddy's dick you start to gyrate
Your hips begging please Daddy dominate
Me like nobody ever has, I need eight
Inches shove it in my mouth, make me suffocate
On your wide dick please really violate
Med Daddy like a wild primate
Be a good girl and demonstrate
What happens as your body starts to levitate
Ask nicely baby girl, say please Daddy dominate.

DRIPPING

She's bathing the dogs and she's dripping
She's laughing, smiling, and grinning
She can't help it the towel starts slipping
She said please sir give me side splitting
Laughter and I start really insisting
You really enjoy drenched dripping
She loves when I say get wenching
She bends over and starts spitting
She's so drenched she starts stripping
Bending over while I start whipping
Her ass she loves firm hitting
It gets her extra saucy, she's totally dripping

DROWNING

She wanted all the cum until she's drowning
In it, she wants a serious ass pounding
All my male friends start surrounding
Her this is a freak show but I'm not clowning
Around she loves cum, especially drowning
In it so many loads she quit counting
She uses me to help with her accounting
More dick, more cum, her lust is outstanding
She loves when everyone starts crowding
Around her so many men start dousing
Her, covering her in cum, she starts shouting
But I filled her throat, she's really drowning
In sin covered in cum she starts mounting
Me and soon she starts howling
She's the filthiest, it's truly astounding
She loves when there's so much cum she's drowning

EXPAND

She loves men that make her mind expand
Especially those that used their hands
To beat her like a filthy woman
She loved her sex lion, he was part man
He gave into her desires and made no demands
He cut through the bullshit like Spam
She reads his poetry and starts to jam
Another finger in herself, his poetry is damn
Hot and she's leaking like a cracked dam
His seduction of her was a simple plan
First lay her down on black sand
Then spend forever licking her priceless clam
He gives her more pleasure than she can stand
Her definition of pleasure keeps having to expand

Explore

No man had ever helped her deeply explore
Her desire to be used like a filthy whore
She enjoyed the pain and begged for more
Please sir throw me on the floor
Use my body, help me explore
New levels of depravity, more hardcore
Treatment I desire you to make me sore
Beat me hard an use every contour
Of my body she says my holes are your
I grabbed her throat and swiftly tore
Her skirt she was wetter than ever before
Her need for roughness we carefully explore

Fingering

I'm on top of her and I'm fingering

Her tight little asshole, for the first time she's remembering

Just how big of a slut she can be, she's glimmering

As I'm biting her ear she starts christening

Me with so much of her juices I'm lingering

In a puddle of nasty now start fingering

Yourself now bitch are you listening

I'm going to show you pleasures you've been missing

I'm going to make you WET bitch, I'm whispering

And pretty soon you'll start figuring

Out I'm a Devil in disguise, I'll leave you simmering

Most guys promise the world, but I'm delivering

You custom filth so you'll really get to fingering

FIREWORKING

She's dynamite and I love her twerking
If I spent the day with you it would be hurting
So good, she's so good at recording
Her hot little pussy, she's serving
Me and it's really hot, it's fireworking
She's giving great head, I started swerving
Suck me in the car, is this turning
You on filthy slut let me start burning
Naughty as fuck nurse my cock needs nursing
Here's my friend, you both can start jerking
Me off on your faces my dick is squirting
I'm exploding in your faces, I'm fireworking

FREAKY

She's reading this and getting so freaky
She loves when I'm extra cheeky
It makes her so very hot and leaky
I'm making it so wet, her hands move so speedy
She enjoys how big I am and how teeny
I make her feel, she's so very needy
Please Daddy, pretty please beat me
She lets me use all her holes freely
She's gagging on my dick, such a greedy
Slut I know how to make her extra freaky
In her ear I whisper the most steamy
Naughty things I'm filling you completely
She's rubbing her magic lamp and I'm her genie
She said you are so original, you talk so uniquely
She dreams of fucking me when she's sleepy
I fuck her while she's asleep, that's pretty freaky

GAGGING

She loves wearing her ball gag, it's happening
Right now she shakes her ass and starts wagging
Her tail soon I'm mercilessly attacking
Her pussy all her juices I'm lapping
Up she creams but I'm laughing
She gets so wet when she's ball gagging
I quickly and roughly start grabbing
Her tits and she starts gasping
What she needs I give her without asking
I'm pinching her hard and start slapping
Her ass, I get her so hot by ball gagging

GAGGING 1

My first move with her is gagging
Her mouth, she's shrieking and gasping
I'm doing what I want, not asking
Her anything just very hard slapping
I'm making it hurt, I'm carefully attacking
Her ass and she keeps backing
Up on me, she's so wet it keeps happening
She needs big dick energy, she's totally gagging
Bark filthy bitch and start wagging
Your tail, I'm quickly strapping
You down and sharply jabbing
My dick in your mouth, your throat is relaxing
I'm beating her ass, I mean really whacking
Her, she enjoys when I keep her gagging

GRABBING

She's very horny and she starts grabbing
My dick saying please start stabbing
Me with your dick Daddy, she's
Shaking her ass and starts slapping
It really hard, she's really whacking
Herself fiercely, she begs to start shagging
She's a hot pet and starts wagging
Her tail, he ass keeps clapping
Another finger on her clit she keeps adding
To her wetness, she's truly gagging
For some great dick she's having
Another orgasm it keeps happening
She keeps touching my dick, she's attacking
Me, she really loves my dick, she's forcefully grabbing

GREAT

I'm really good, but I strive to be great
I want to make you continuously masturbate
You deserve a man that can fascinate
You, I start with your lips and fixate
My attention on eight hundred licks, that's a hundred times eight
I think eating you would make me lose weight
You open your legs and release a floodgate
Of your essence, your whole body begins to gyrate
And on my dick I can feel you pulsate
What about you is my favorite trait?
Duh, it's gotta be that amazing cake
You are prettier than any Playboy Playmate
I really want to stick it in your tailgate
You deserve a man that knows how to communicate
With his tongue and makes her feel great
I want to totally wreck you, let's copulate
We can take turns on how best to dominate
Your body this poetic heavyweight
Is trying to help really motivate
You to keep going, keep going baby, feel great

GRINDING

You're in my lap and you start slowly grinding
On my dick fast forward then keep rewinding
You let me grope, you aren't minding
The attention I'm striking your clit like lightning
Surrender bitch there's no use in fighting
You love getting juicy from my writing
I make your body happy and shining
Touch yourself and you'll be finding
New sensations and the pleasures will be spell binding
And the colors with be brightly blinding
I know right now you can't help sliding
Your fingers in, I know you are grinding

Heart

I know just the right way to kick start
Your passions, let me make pleasure an art
Lay back and let your legs begin to part
I'll give you desires you never knew were in your heart
Your body is a dartboard and my tongue quickly darts
To your ass, I'll have to carry you away in a cart
Leaving you a puddle of filth, I'll tear you apart
I'm a super patient man, that's a smart
Way to show a woman the quality of my heart

Horniest

Sexy unicorns make me the horniest
They make my canvas fill with zest
Making her squirt is a really good test
She was horny and started to guess
What she's fondling her cute breasts
I knew I could make her the horniest
Let me eat you while you rest
I want to win the pie eating contest
She said you horniness makes me impressed
Licking her body I cuff her you're under arrest
Do you have any last requests?
She whispered please Daddy make me the horniest
Unicorn ever her juices explode on my face, I'm refreshed
Making her squirt screaming I'm so blessed
Cover your unicorn, you are the absolute best
She begs now please finish on my chest!

Horny Squirting Slut

You're a self-proclaimed horny squirting slut
You love making the filthiest smut
She begs Daddy please stick it in my butt
Please destroy me like a fucking slut
Giving it to her the hardest, she's just
One of many horny squirting sluts
That use my words to give them what
They really want which is to touch their cunt
Her mouth is never allowed to shut
On your knees and smile like a doughnut
Imagine a Maui vacation, I feed you coconuts
You love showing off your beautiful bust
Let me show you what's beyond lust
Touch yourself now, you horny squirting slut

HORSE

She's a nasty cowgirl and I'm her horse
She rides me with great hip action and force
She begs me to prolong our intercourse
She said you truly are the source
Of all this wetness, I'm a slut soaked horse
I'd like to take you on a golf course
And get a hole in one with all sorts
She rocks on top of me I fully support
Her I'm her oak and she feels no remorse
About riding the shit out of her filthy horse
Giddy up nasty cowgirl, do your worst

Hunting

She admired my excellent word hunting
How I could say almost nothing
Yet with a whisper make her feel something
So incredible, the blood is rushing
Straight to her brain as her heart starts pumping
She knew the beast was coming
She was his prey and tonight he was hunting
He called out there's no use in running
Princess I'll give you what you are wanting
I'll be your cement pogo stick start jumping
For joy you've finally found someone that enjoys fucking
As much as you and start trusting
That I'll make your panties leak as the liquid starts rushing
Down your legs I go balls deep, you knew it was coming
I stick it in your ass and right as I'm cumming
You stick it in your mouth that's something
Nasty I know you enjoy the more disgusting
I am with you the hotter the fucking
Now you don't have a prayer I'm thrusting
Wildly, you are caught in my snare I'm hunting

IMAGINING

I get her pussy so wet she's imagining
Me and her pussy keeps dampening
She's like Daddy look at what's happening
She wants me to be her doctor and start examining
Her pussy, is it as wet as I'm imagining
She gives into desire, there's no battling
Her desires, she's using her hand it's challenging
But I spit on her and start strangling
Her she loves extra rough handling
Daddy your big dick energy is so fascinating
I'm in her mind fucking scrambling
Her ovaries, she's like I'm practicing
Being the biggest slut, filthier than you're imagining

INCH

She begged him to explore every inch
Of her between pain and pleasure he would switch
He threw her in the bottom of a ditch
She loved being treated like a filthy bitch
He smacked her so hard and she didn't flinch
She loved how he would roughly pinch
Her nipples it felt like Christmas and he was the Grinch
He was the greatest explorer, he explored every inch
He was her dark and twisted prince
He showered with her juices, he started to rinse
Her essence off him laughing so easy to convince
Her he made her body shudder and wince
He tied her up and used her as his wench
He was not gentle when he sticks his monkey wrench
In her and it completely fills her, every inch

JUICE

She wants to smother me with her juice
She's created a wild lion that's now loose
I'm making her squawk like a goose
All her holes are for my use
She loves when I beat her body, loves the abuse
It makes her pussy leak lots of juice
She's wearing fishnets and thigh high boots
I'm grabbing her hair roughly by the roots
She's always horny, always down to reproduce
My tongue is so deep in her hot caboose
I'm bottling her wetness and drinking it as juice

Kitty

She enjoys men that are witty
A great personality is a really
Big turn on I think she's super pretty
She shakes her ass so fast it makes me dizzy
She's bending over in a skirt that's mini
Oh my goodness she just flashed me her kitty
It appears I've made her quite wet and sticky
She grabs my head and says lick your kitty
She wants it rough, she needs it quickly
Please sir, please stick it in me
Her hands are so fast and busy
She's curvaceous yet skinny
I'm her Kermit, she's my Miss Piggy
She's reading this and touching her kitty

Knees

She happily and quickly is on her knees
She begs Daddy pretty please
She's very sensually starting a striptease
She's showing off her expertise
She's fingering herself with such ease
It makes he so wet being on her knees
She's a huge slut a d knows just how to tease
Me handcuffed and gagged she hands me the keys
She wants me to destroy her body, she's like these
Tits, ass, and pussy are totally free
To do whatever you like she wants the filthiest sleaze
She's the hottest cat and I'm her cheese
She's jumping for joy, my dick is the trapeze
She's very, very hot and I'm her breeze
She's gagging for it when I say beg bitch, on your knees

Know

How do I know what you need it's
So obvious you need a guy
That makes you do what most wouldn't try
In the theatre you unzip my fly
You grab my hand and push it between your thighs
You said sir you are very wise
Then she revealed her own little surprise
Nice butt plug she shakes and feeds me fries
It's obvious that extra-large is her favorite size
She said would you help me tie
Myself up and give me what you know
I need, she's like treat me like a filthy ho
Grab my hair, spank me, throw
Me around and cut off my blood flow
Choke me Daddy and take me where nobody else dares to go
I'm shoving my cock down her throat, she's so
Fucking filthy and she's ready to blow
Me again as she quickly begins to make me grow
You're the biggest slut, we both know

LEAK

I'm making this filthy slut's pussy leak
She's roughly pinching her nipples, rough tweaks
Her pussy is so wet I can hear it squeak
She loves the way that I speak
To her like a fucking filthy freak
Being treated like a total whore makes her leak
She needs a real man to abuse her physique
She wants it roughly, she wants me to beat
My words get her soaking, she loves my technique
I'm shoving my dick in her cheek
She's getting so hot she starts to shriek
Her room smells like sex, it really reeks
Of cum, it makes her pussy so very weak
She loves my words, they are so unique
I know just how to make this superfreak
Make a huge puddle, I'm really making her leak

LEAKING

She's a bitch in heat, she's always leaking
She begs please choke me hard so I'm not speaking
I'm giving it to her, just what she's needing
My entire dick in her mouth, I'm feeding
Her most favorite treat, she's really screaming
Now and the bed is soaked, she's totally creaming
The heat from her pussy is steaming
Up the camera and she keeps leaking
Over the microphone but she's sneaking
Glances like when will Daddy be needing
Me to be his fucktoy again, she's leaking
And I'm filling her holes, she's been dreaming
Of dominant dick in her mouth, it keeps her leaking

LEGLESS

She asked me to fuck her legless
I think you're dick drunk what are you trying to express
She said you make me want to confess
That I'm the biggest slut and I say lift your dress
I know how voracious your appetite gets
You beg me to let you wear less
Daddy please make my panties an amazing mess
I want you to start rubbing your fantastic breasts
Your legs glide open giving full access
My tongue gives you pleasure to excess
Nothing succeeds like sexcess
I deliver pleasure quicker than Federal Express
I'm not playing bitch, this isn't recess
I'm going to fuck you so senseless
I'll have to carry you like you are legless

LIKE

She said thank you sir and she would like
Me to take control and aggressively write
Her body is so firm and so ripe
She enjoys my hand around her throat tight
I'm giving it to her just how she would like
She gets wet when I start to strike
Her ass and make her ride me like a bike
Treating her dirty is the right
Way to get her horny and excite
We're both huge sluts, so alike
I'm getting her hot to her delight
She says thank you sir, I truly like

Lyft

I want to make you Uber hot, so I say lift
Your skirt higher and show me your gift
The perfectly wrapped package I insist
You lay back and let me slowly kiss
Your neck and slap your perfect tits
I'm going to dominate you and get
You soaking wet, you'll have to pay Lyft
A cleaning fee cause you literally dripped
All over the seat a puddle of filth it barely fit
In your beautiful mouth and I ripped
Your pantyhose and my tongue is swift
To give satisfaction I will hit
You so deeply you will beg me to desist
I'm pounding it hard let me assist
You in getting you wet, I'm driving for Lyft

MADE

She loves being commanded so he made
Her bend over and her hips swayed
She loved the words how he would degrade
Her nasty bitch she naughtily played
With her body and she knew she gave
Him hardness that really made
Her horny so did how he replayed
Her being a slut, she dressed as a maid
Her leaking pussy totally betrayed
Her whore nature she was afraid
To be a total bitch but he would persuade
Her to touch herself, grab her braids
She submitted eagerly, she loves being made

MAN

You make me want to evolve as a man
Lifting you to new heights, expanding your wingspan
Saying wow how does it get better than
That, I'll tell you I'm your biggest fan
That you're worthy of the very best man
I'm not sure exactly when it all began
But I think it's when you said you're the man
She confessed I think about you while using my hand
You give me pleasure so good, please can
You get it juicy for me, I'll grab a drip pan
I'll make you melt in my mouth in the span
Of a few minutes, you beg me fuck me like a caveman
Grab my hair, choke me, fuck me hard man
I'm sucking you pleasurably, I'm your quicksand
Imagine leaking all over Hawaiian black sand
Beaches, is this sounding like a good plan?

MEAT

She wants me to treat her like a piece of fucking meat
Grabbing her by the hair the instant we meet
Doing dirty things make her leak
She's a grade A certified freak
She greedily swallows my thick meat
Her hot ass I roughly start to beat
She's giving into temptation, she's so weak
Daddy has her most favorite treat
Daddy please destroy your fuck meat
She's flashing me in the middle of the street
She's like please give me that sweet
Meat Daddy please really mistreat
My body by beating me hard, increase the heat
She likes when I put it on her as hard as concrete
Yes Daddy, use me like a piece of fucking meat

MERCY

She wants me to make her beg for mercy
I put her firmly over my knee
Her eyes reveal her lustful glee
She's so excited she started to pee
Tonight there will be no mercy
I don't care how loud her plea
I'm going to fuck all three
Of her holes, she's tied up and I'm free
To be my authentic self, I'm beastly
I'm beating her ass like a horse at the derby
Tonight we are going on an exciting, dark journey
I'm going to break this bitch, she's not sturdy
She begs me for cum, she's so thirsty
She says Daddy I'm starting to worry
That you'll make me do things most dirty
Dirtiest things ever I laugh as I'm in no hurry
I've got all night slut as I bite her perky
Breasts she cries out she's scared of my fury
She should be, tonight there will be no mercy

Missing

My heart rejoices with you I'm missing
You but not the canvas I'm dripping
My essence like you cause such Thanksgiving
Before you I wasn't really living
And now you'll receive the best gifting
With my tongue not an inch will be missing
Where did your clothes go I thought you were slipping
Into something more comfortable but damn winning
Savoring every drop of you I'm sipping
Unicorn tears you keep misting
Me with your juices it's getting
Very juicy I wish you'd start pissing
All over me I love naughty sinning
You love it fucking filthy, you're listening
Carefully I grab your hair and start twisting
Your pleasure spot I keep hitting
You love naughty words they are getting
You super horny your panties I'm sniffing
Smells like cherries swallow me, no spitting
Take my whole length in your mouth until it goes missing

MOOD

She enjoyed that I always get her in the mood
She was hungry, but not for food,
She loves when I'm nasty and lewd
She enjoys when I'm cunning and shrewd
Wait I mean when I'm cumming this dude
Really knows how to get her attitude
Like fuck me please that's the mood
She doesn't lock her phone and sends nude
Photos like Daddy I'm so not prude
I'm the biggest slut and she shows gratitude
By showing things that she would usually exclude
But the way I see how her clit starts to protrude
And now I'm on her clit like I'm glued
I'll suck your soul through your ass, that's my mood

MORE

Dress like a maid and get on the floor
You make my dick really roar
You're the sexiest, freakiest whore
And though you can't ask for more
I'm going to keep making your pussy sore
I know you're touching yourself, I know your
Weakness is my tongue in your backdoor
Today I'm giving you ass slaps galore
So much filthy touching, you really start to pour
Your juices are leaking more than before
You cum, I want you to beg for more
I'll leash you and walk you outdoors
Licking my dick is your favorite chore
You enjoy it fast, rough, and really hardcore
Daddy brought you a friend, ok actually four
Service us all slut, take it some more

MOVIE

I took this bad girl to a movie
She thinks I'm super groovy
While the lights were still on she blew me
I need the lights to enjoy her beauty
That and to properly smack her booty
She's reading this and getting very juicy
She's on fire bubbling like a Jacuzzi
She said give me that big, fruity
Snack her shirt hanging on loosely
I'm in the movies with a total floozie
She's not the type I'd call choosy
I'm firing on all cylinders with my uzi
She and I are making our own movie

MOVIE STAR

She said we all can't look like a movie star
It made me laugh out loud like are
You being serious, she is totally bizarre
She says I'm ridiculous, in my memoir
I'll say I'm a lighter and she's a cigar
She's smoking hot, she's a movie star
She's a total mermaid, I'm a sandbar
I'm her cracker, she's my caviar
Spreading all over me I've got a huge repertoire
She's the Cookie Monster and I'm a cookie jar
Why don't we go in the backseat of your car
And make a naughty video, my movie star

Naughty Surprise

Thank you baby for my naughty surprise
You've got such a great ass and thighs
I really enjoy how high your skirt flies
Damn baby that milkshake is cool want fries
You have the loveliest blue eyes
May I help your temperature rise
I'll use ropes and start to verbalize
The way I'm holding you down with zip ties
Forcing my whole length makes you see skies
The wetness I carefully surmise
Oh that pussy is getting so wet look at the size
Of that puddle I give her such butterflies
Fucking her in public is such a naughty surprise

NAUGHTY

How many people make you feel really naughty
Your body is kicking like karate
I want you to squeeze your body
And imagine being blindfolded while somebody
Just spends forever licking your most naughty
Parts I enjoy pleasing women it's my hobby
I especially like it when you bend over doggie
Style I'd start fingering you in the hotel lobby
You are absolutely sensational, my favorite hottie
I'll get you so wet, I'm talking really sloppy
You deserve an expert tongue, let's get naughty

NEEDING

I worship her; it is what she is needing
She said please, she's really pleading
She deserves it all so I'm feeding
Her soul and her body is seething
I desire to give her pleasure without ceasing
I'm behind her and I'm slowly eating
Her ass and she keeps leaking
She touches herself when reading
My words she uses her mouth to start beating
My dick up she's cleaning
My cock with her gorgeous hair I'm dreaming
I'd do anything to keep her steaming
She had never had a man start speaking
To her so sweetly, it's exactly what she's needing.

Nursing

How does it get better than her nursing
She loves touching herself and is yearning
To show me new pleasures she is learning
How to be head nurse she's been working
Really hard to touch herself to my flirting
She took my temperature with her mouth, that's excellent nursing
My pleasure and my needs are what she's concerning
Herself with tonight she starts twerking
On my face until she starts squirming
I lick her clit until she starts squirting
All over my face, her inner freak is emerging
She is the nastiest nurse, she keeps nursing
My cock in her mouth like this wording
Dear slut suck my dick the size keeps worsening
My balls are full here's what you are deserving
Of another breakfast for her, she loves sinful nursing

Pet

I know this super kinky, fiery brunette
And I know just how to make her wet
She loves being collared, she loves being my pet
She loves when I yank her chain, it makes her sweat
She's dripping down her torn fishnets
Reading this part she starts to pet
Herself, she's slowly smoking a cigarette
In the Jacuzzi she's rubbing the jet
She loves being collared it really does get
Her so horny, this guy on the internet
Makes her wish to be my pet

PISSING

She really loves when I let her start pissing
On me she's starting off by misting
Me then it pours out she's hissing
Daddy tell me the nastiest things I'm listening
She shoves her panties on my face I'm sniffing
Her soaked panties, she's glistening
Love when she is nasty and starts pissing
All over me there's no use in resisting
Making her so hot her hips start twisting
Her asshole with my tongue I'm tickling
Her fancy self I don't give a fuck I'm sipping
Her piss, she's really sensing
That this guys isn't missing
A single drop, she's wishing
I'd piss all over her, she's like is it Thanksgiving
Cause she wants to be stuffed are you listening
Slut my mouth is open, start pissing

Please

She gagged herself and let me do as I please
I grab her hair and yank her on her knees
Making her pussy drenched with such ease
She needed to be Daddy dick dominated with expertise
Pinching her nipples makes her freeze
Oh Daddy make it hurt so badly please
I lock her up and throw away the keys
I'm going to very slowly and hotly tease
Her, she loves my filthy sleaze
I slap her tits, they are mine these
She's hot as hell and I blow her body with breeze
She's begging put it in Daddy, pretty please

POSITION

She asked would you fuck me in this position
I'm a certified freak on a mission
With one thing on my mind, making you glisten
Your ass and my dick that's an interesting proposition
I'll leave you in a puddle of fucked up condition
Having her doing things she can never mention
I'll beat that ass up, total demolition
I'll make you forget any inhibition
I'm making it burn, she loves the friction
She gets so wet reading the things I have written
The way I pound her with forceful precision
She's saying Jesus Christ like she's caught religion
I'm her doctor and I'm writing a prescription
Turn on a video of you and your girlfriend on the television
Handcuff yourself like you're in prison
Gagging you so I don't have to listen
To your screams, I'm making it disappear like a magician
Face down, ass up, that's my favorite position

Prize

This morning when I opened my eyes
I was in for quite the surprise
I tell no tales and these are no lies
I woke up to the hottest prize
The bed was filled with French fries
She walked in like with a sex drive that size
Her milkshake brings many ladies and most guys
She's oozing super freak, and it's super sized
She opens her fur coat, and out flies butterflies
She's like come kneel in between my thighs
She whispers it's not sex, it's exercise
Her red lips really tantalize
With devil horns she's like come demonize
Me let's make light and really epitomize
Hot stuff, hands off the merchandise
She's always dressing up in some disguise
She laughs and then breaks out the zip ties
Lay back and let me make your dick cry
She purposefully aims it in her eyes
She licks it up, it's her favorite size

Punishing

She really enjoyed the most when he was punishing
Her, it made her pussy start running
Like a river he kept her cumming
Like a bad girl she said Daddy please more punishing
She loves when he starts roughly touching
Her ass because she knows what's coming
Red ass today baby, she's really loving
Being put in her place, she's stuffing
Two fingers in her hungry pussy quietly grunting
He wants to make this bitch in heat start yelping
She quickly starts licking and rubbing
Herself, she cares about nothing
But being bad, she's so stunning
Baby does this get it juicy for you, are you gushing?

RAIL

She really desired to have him rail
Her and she said Daddy please impale
Me bang me with your hammer, really nail
It she shakes her hot little tail
She wants to be a total slut, to get really railed
I beat her roughly, she's not frail
I make her soaking wet without fail
She's a princess, but this is a naughty fairytale
Her body is a Ferrari and I carefully detail
Every inch with my tongue I inhale
Her sweetness, her juices are my favorite cocktail
She shreds my back with her fingernails
I'm running a train on her until she gets derailed
I'm her large, powerful Clydesdale
I choke her so that she can't exhale
I'm her naughty prince and I assail
Her body, she loves when I totally rail
Her Daddy hurts it so good she's a nasty female
Nothing pleases her more than getting railed

RAINBOW

I was dreaming, watching colors flow
My excitement started to grow
In her hands stroking me nice and slow
She looked into my eyes and said oh
Daddy would you let me taste the rainbow
She said cover me in your color so
Much color she said draw me a photo
She makes me horny as a rhino
With her feminine curves and sexy torso
My body feels like it hit the lotto
I'll paint her face like I'm Van Gogh
She starts increasing her tempo
She said the moon is in Scorpio
I'm starting to leak, starting to overflow
She uses her mouth and hands like a pro
Begging please Daddy, I need to taste your rainbow

RED BOTTOMS

I have a date idea that involves red bottoms
We go to Neiman Marcus and buy you a paid of Christian Louboutin
You say Daddy you really spoil me rotten
Ah dear it seems you have forgotten
That now I'm going to give you a red bottom
She said please spank me hard, that would be awesome
She whispered, I hope you punish me quite often
I could really use another pair of red bottoms.

REINDEER

She's dressing up like a sexy reindeer
She's so horny it's weird
She loves my tongue deep in her rear
As I fill her mouth out drops a tear
Of joy, I fill her body with cheer
She's a very, very horny reindeer
She sits on my lap begging come here
Daddy please rail me with your spear
I'm going to cum on her face and smear
It was a nasty cum soaked reindeer

ROUGH

I show her my strength, how tough
I am and immediately start being rough
Hands behind her back, I click the handcuffs
Bark like a dog bitch, let me hear you ruff
I choke her and she can't get enough
She's a bitch in heat and I start to stuff
Her ass, I pause, and then start to thrust
I'm pounding her and you can trust
The camera is rolling, she's such a slut
I do things to her that really disgust
Her the filthier, the more lust
Take it slut, I'm deep in her butt
Fuck Daddy, she gets slapped, I said not to cuss
And I slap the shit out of her cute bust
Nothing makes her drip like playing rough

Rubbing

She said I'm the nastiest and started rubbing
Herself in the bathtub she's scrubbing
Herself dirty, she said give me nasty loving
I'm in her ass slowly pumping
Her full and she's quickly shoving
Another finger in herself she's touching
Herself reading this and she's stuffing
Herself like a Thanksgiving turkey there's nothing
That she won't do, she's the nastiest, she's coming
Back for more pleasure, her juices are flooding
She said I'm addictive and she's drugging
Herself and my balls she's gently cupping
Them with her mouth she starts hugging
My dick, soon I'll be cumming
Everywhere and she'll start running
To catch every drop, she's really something
Else and she just can't stop her naughty rubbing

SECRET

Right away I knew her deepest secret
She plays coy and I'll never forget
That her most favorite treat
Is sneaking away for a hot little treat
She enjoys casually getting pounded by meat
So many men she kind of forgets
All of them so many nasty secrets
When she starts to quickly pet
Herself thinking her only regret
Is she wished she'd get more wet
With total transparency when we met
I was like she gives incredible neck
What a little whore, she's got a secret

SEDUCE

She was a filthy whore at her roots
He knew exactly how to reduce
Her to a puddle of leaky juice
She had never had someone seduce
Her so eloquently, his expert use
Of words was able to quickly induce
Her consent as he slapped her caboose
She desires firm, powerful abuse
When he told her how he would seduce
Her it made her want to reproduce
He's stuffing her like a Christmas goose
She scream oh God, he says call me Zeus
He's using his hand like a noose
Choking her wildly he really lets loose
The animal inside her, he's a mental masseuse
Massaging her brain was the best way to seduce

SIN

She encouraged his inner demon
She said angle it's ok to sin
She knew exactly what she wanted from him
He came through the door and then
Grabbed her hands and made her spin
Around against the wall he started to pin
Her down oh goody she needed a lesson
In depravity and he was ready to sin
Being treated firmly made her glisten
She enjoyed this side of her friend
She yelped as he firmly slapped her rear end
As his hands groped her skin
Her desire, her moisture would begin
To leak uncontrollably, she fucking loves sin

Skirt

She slowly starts to lift her skirt
She loves showing him her flirt
He said filthy bitch, he says you're dirt
It made her so wet she starts to squirt
Leaving a damp patch on her skirt
She loved how passionately he hurt
Her body the pressure he would exert
Her neck being choked got her alert
When he commanded her to insert
A finger and let him taste dessert
She was a naughty, filthy pervert
It got her so wet under her skirt

Slapping

She secretly desires rough slapping
When his large hands start wrapping
Around her throat and he starts attacking
Her body, her hair he's tightly grabbing
As he starts hotly and firmly slapping
Her she starts dripping when he's paddling
Her she gets so damp as he's whacking
Her body across the floor he's dragging
Her and the sound of his belt cracking
Against her body makers her start jabbing
Fingers Inside the juices grow as he's smacking
Her she desires the roughest slapping

Sneak

She loves being tricky, she loves to sneak
It is obvious to me she's a total freak
The quickest and easiest way to make her leak
Is to start grabbing her hot asscheeks
And stick your dick in her cheek
She's up for it, as long as you sneak
Around she's always wet and weak
When you start to slowly speak
About how tricky and sleek
She is and you're especially unique
I'll keep it a secret, love when you sneak

So Good

I want to take you beyond so good
Let's be bad little red riding hood in the woods
I'm the Big Bad Wolf and you understood
That you'll soon me in my mouth so good
She loves sucking on my hard redwood
The thick trunk really hits her clitoris hood
Perfectly, she deserves to have her womanhood
Served and eaten forever if I could
Just lick your neck, she whispers could
You please stick it in my ass, bury your manhood
Deep I'm the gasoline to your firewood
I make her pussy feel oh so good

SOAKING

Imagine being in the bath happily soaking
She says please Daddy I'm not joking
Please grab me by the hair and start choking
Me she sees me and tries stroking
Me but I say no and it's provoking
Quite and interesting reaction, it makes her start soaking
Her panties reading this like love where this is going
She says you're so inventive and thought provoking
I love when her nipples start poking
Out it's the first stage in intense soaking
I'm making her so hot she starts smoking
I'm in between her legs lightly blowing
She uses her fingers to rapidly start probing
Herself, she's a dog in heat, her juices are flowing
She thanks me for keeping her exploding
She smiles, this is just what I was hoping
For thanks sir for keeping me soaking

SOME MORE

She said I truly couldn't ask for more
I said let me lick your spiritual core
Let me ignite your lava and watch it pour
All over me as I start whispering, your allure
Makes me rise to levels most pure
You love when I put you on all fours
You touch yourself so much, it's a little sore
I'll keep your secrets, I truly adore
You, you're more beautiful than Hawaii seashells on the shore
Bringing you pleasure is a topic I'd like to explore
Let me lick your pleasure button some more
Let me lick your body until you can't ignore
The itch is growing your mind fills with impure
Thoughts like, I wish he'd respectfully treat me like his whore
I'm shooting my shot, did I score?

Song

It was music to her ears my horny song
She got so damp she already moved her thong
She said be fucking filthy, sing something wrong
Lick my pleasure button as I prolong
Her orgasms she said nobody ever made me a song
Men that were kind and vulnerable were strong
Men that focused on her squirting make her break into song
She's gagging for dick, she really wants my schlong
She's thinking of licking my dong
I know just where my tongue belongs
Making her squirt uncontrollably all day long
She's making a puddle a mile long
Puddle pussy that's the name of this song

Sound

Her pussy is so wet it's making a squeaky sound
It gets her horny when I push her face to the ground
She likes the way I roughly toss her around
She spreads her ass and begs me to pound
It gag yourself bitch, don't make a sound
Smacking her ass so big and round
Shoving my dick in her mouth on the playground
She is leaking I just found
Her wet panties she turned around
And without any warning I heard the sound
Of her clicking handcuffs, I love that sound
Now my face is buried in her mound
She's a queen and I carefully crowned
Her with my cum there's plenty to go around
She's choking on my dick, my favorite sound

SPECIALIST

She said I really need my specialist
He fills me with the naughtiest
Thoughts and discovers new pleasures that exist
She touches herself so much she has a sprained wrist
She can't stop touching her, she can't resist
He's licking her brain with amazing twists
He's in her ass more than proctologist
She needed to cum, he would always happily assist
Lay back and receive I insist
On her neck I lightly begin to kiss
She's soaking now, she needed her specialist

Squirming

She wants me to feel her squirming
On my dick, between her thighs she is yearning
For someone to help her experience learning
I'm setting fire to her crotch, it's working
Reading this she really starts squirming
She gives a lot so I start serving
Her nonstop thrusts, I'm earning
A place in her bed with sexy flirting
Baby let me give you what you have been searching
For a worthy man that consistently is stirring
Her juices and when I put it all in she starts squirting
Slapping her ass, she loves it burning
Hot baby does this make you start squirming?

SUBMISSION

She begged for it, she loves submission
She likes being slapped, being bitten
Treat me so nasty she said you have permission
Make me hurt so bad it's her mission
To make him her mast, her submission
Was complete she released all inhibition
Being a fucking whore was her secret addiction
She gasped he moved her in a position
Of vulnerability she would obediently listen
I'll do anything sir, happily she chooses submission

SUCKER

I'm a demon, a true soul sucker
I'm a freak and I'm undercover
I'm the naughtiest, filthiest lover
I love when your outfit is made of rubber
Orgasms please she says please another
She started to speak but now she can't utter
A word I suck the soul out of her vagina another
Demon satisfied and I spit it back in her mouth no other
Guy has done that for her she's starting to shudder
My face is a hot pan and her pussy is butter
She's dripping all over me like a Texas summer
She brought her friend and begged me to fuck her
I'm deep in her ass now, I'm a slutty sucker

Surrender

I am devilishly tempting, she will surrender
To my advances growling come hither
She gasps with the force that I enter
Her and I'm really stretching her innards
She quickly start shoving her finger
In her ass into temptation slut surrender
I make her go on a dick bender
More and more dick, I'm her dick bartender
I take away her breath, I'm a contender
Choking my whore not being at all tender
She fucks random guys she meets on Tinder
She wants it deep in her fender
My tongue on her clit, right on the center
She creams Daddy please, I fucking surrender!

Suspense

She was frightened and excited, the suspense
Of being tied with a chain to the fence
Put in her place ever since
She submitted he kept her in such suspense
The way the beatings he would dispense
Made her shudder, made her wince
He knew what she wanted, he could sense
Her desire to be beat she made no defense
The way he hit her with energy so intense
His hands made her juices puddle in an immense
Pool nothing got her wetter than great suspense

SWELLING

She touches her pussy so much it's swelling
She said would you mind telling
Me something gripping and compelling
Make my insides start melting
My tongue is slowly dwelling
On your backside and you start yelping
Let your body and brain start really swelling
With naughty thoughts I'll keep spelling
Out how I'd worship you, the pleasure is overwhelming
I just want to make you really start sweating
You just lay back and slowly start spreading
Your ass I hope this is really helping
You get super wet, enjoy my naughty storytelling

TINY

I'm so big and strong, she's so tiny
She like it wild and rough, I'm mighty
Wild tonight I'm fucking her deep in her psyche
She quit counting orgasms after ninety
I'm filling her completely, she's so tiny
Baby girl loves when I treat her body unkindly
I'm spanking her ass bent over my knee
I ignore all her cries, her cute little pleas
I'm railing her and stretching her tiny
Mouth, she cries tears of glee
She's so scared, like I think he
Might seriously fucking break me
Put another finger inside slut, make it three
She's like I can't get it in Daddy
I'm ripping her wide open, she's so tiny

Touching

She couldn't help continuously touching
Herself, she loves his sensual loving
She needed his words, she keeps cumming
Harder and faster, her juices are running
Down her leg, he's got the magic touch, he's touching
Her so pleasantly, she's wearing next to nothing
With her blindfolded his tongue starts running
Down her lower back, her dampness is becoming
Serious, she says I love how you keep touching
Me so well please keep munching
In between my legs, he's quickly brushing
Her clit and he's focused on never rushing
Sir you are seriously so fucking
Good, I'm drenched, you make me start touching
Myself as she uses two fingers to start stuffing
She loves when he keeps tongue hugging
Her ass, showing him how she keeps touching

WALL

I'm going to press your face against the wall
No resistance today, none at all
She loves when I make her inhibitions fall
She feels so powerless and small
In my arms she enjoys how tall
I am when she needs pleasure she will call
Me and say please shove me against a wall
Be a sexy beast and roughly maul
Me, she likes the naughty pictures I draw
Her in closer and she's like you're my alcohol
You get me drunk with pleasure I can't recall
Anyone that has made me wetter she makes a catcall
I'm licking her soul, pleasing her eyeballs
I don't think she can fit both my balls
In her mouth but she's my happy sex doll
She lets me do anything I want, it makes her bawl
It feels so good for her to be taken against the wall

WATCHING

She could feel his eyes watching
Her as she slowly started washing
When she starts expertly dropping
To her knees it gets her absolutely sopping
His dick deep in her throat watching
Her eyes tear up as he's flogging
Her hot ass she's his filthy plaything
She is always touching herself, there's no stopping
The puddle he makes her start mopping
It up with her tongue as he's watching

WHATEVER

The hottest devil on Onlyfans offered me whatever
I want and now I'm pulling the lever
To soak her incredibly, she's never
Been so soaked, hardest orgasm ever
I whisper you truly deserve better
I want you in a mask of leather
My tongue hits your clit with the lightest pressure
As I tickle your ass with a peacock feather
You're the best, a true sparkling treasure
I love to hotly surprise you, I'm a ghost pepper
Let me spice things up until you surrender whatever
You want sir nobody writes fresher
Making women wet, the best trendsetter
You're the cutest Minnie Mouse and I've got lots of cheddar

WHERE

She said I wonder exactly where
He's going to touch me, hopefully somewhere
Sensitive he starts licking her through her underwear
He pops his head up truth or dare
Truth you can stick it in anywhere
Dare you to go rough he grabs her hair
Over his knee sitting on a chair
Smack, smack, smack, she's dripping everywhere
She sees him recording but she doesn't care
Her senses are awakening, she's more aware
Of the deliciousness of their secret affair
I'll touch you in spots where
You love and you're in my mouth beware
I'm doing so good it makes her swear
She's surprised how nasty I get her where
She can tell he did a lot to prepare
The wolf whispering to the sheep come into my lair
When you leave you're going to need a wheelchair

WHORE

She loves being the filthiest whore
She likes being really dirty then doing more
She loves being pushed down and pounded on the floor
She prefers multiple cocks, hopefully today four
Men fill her throat, she says I've never done this before
Quit lying girl, we all know you're a filthy whore
Letting strangers finger you on the dance floor
You love sex, you suck dick with such vigor
Get over here I can't take it anymore
I've got your favorite present little whore
Tonight we are going to really explore
Your limits in your Hooters outfit doing chores
You like it rough, you enjoy it hardcore
I'm fucking your face, my scandalous little whore.

WIDE

She's opening herself up very wide
Two toys she sticks inside
Her, she's got a whole collection by her bedside
She enjoys how wet she gets, she slides
Another finger in her mouth to provide
Me with stimulation, open your mouth wide
She said nobody has ever tried
To make her pussy and mid collide
I'm licking her super-hot backside
She's the nastiest slut, there's no way to hide
That much filth, she's looking at me cockeyed
Wait I mean I just came in her eye
Open your mouth slut, open very wide

WORSHIPPING

I'm at her alter and I'm worshipping
I'm in her secret garden harvesting
I'm long term material, no interest in a fling
I'm lovingly licking her until she sings
Oh man she really needed divine worshipping
She's totally open, letting me do anything
She said you're an angel without the wing
Or you're the devil she can't think of a thing
But her excitement at my hardening
She unzips me and whispers darling
You're a magician, she's marveling
She's swallowing me like she's starving
So much gagging, so much worshipping

Yes Sir

With a gasp, she happily said yes sir
She loved what he did to her
It made her very hot and she would pur
At the longings and desires he would stir
He called her a filthy bitch and that slur
Motivated her deeply, it would spur
Longings inside the wetness would occur
The powerful way he would refer
To her as a nasty slut let her transfer
All power, she loved submitting, yes sir

www.ingramcontent.com/pod-product-compliance
Lightning Source LLC
Chambersburg PA
CBHW060335260626
47160CB00007B/2799